GRANADOS

12 SPANISH DANCES OPUS 5 FOR THE PIANO

EDITED BY OLGA LLANO KUEHL-WHITE

CONTENTS

This volume is lovingly dedicated to all future pianists, to enlighten and to delight them.

—Olga Llano Kuehl-White

Copyright © 2012 by Alfred Music
All rights reserved. Produced in USA.
ISBN-10: 0-7390-7910-7
ISBN-13: 978-0-7390-7910-2

Cover art: Dance on the Banks of the River Manzanares, *1777*
by Francisco Jose de Goya y Lucientes (1746-1828)
Oil on canvas
Prado, Madrid, Spain

ABOUT THE COMPOSER

Enrique Granados y Campiña—composer, pianist and teacher—created a rich musical legacy with his piano compositions, which are held in high esteem by musicians worldwide. He was born in the Catalán city of Lérida, Spain on July 27,1867. His mother, Enriqueta Alvira Campiña, was from Santander in northern Spain, and his father, Calixto Granados Armenteros (a captain in the Spanish army), was of Spanish descent but born in Cuba. After a short military assignment in Lérida, the family moved to the Canary Islands, where Granados's father was stationed for three years as the Military Governor. By 1874, the family had moved to Barcelona, the Catalán capital, which was renowned for its cultural and educational opportunities that embraced all areas of artistic endeavors. Granados began musical studies with a family friend, Captain José Junqueda, and later with Francesc Jurnet, another teacher of limited abilities. Fortunately, by 1880, Granados became a student of Joan Baptista Pujol (1835–1898). Pujol was a graduate of the Paris Conservatory, a composer-pianist and a published author of a piano method entitled *A New Approach to Piano Technique*.

In 1884, Granados began harmony and composition studies with Felipe Pedrell (1841–1922). As a composer, teacher and musicologist, Pedrell had transcribed hundreds of regional folk tunes, initiating a musical renaissance in Spain. He urged all his composition students to embrace Spanish Nationalism and celebrate its indigenous folk music. Granados always acknowledged Pedrell's profound influence in his artistic and philosophical development. By 1886, upon his father's death, Granados sought work as a café pianist, out of financial necessity. Before long, he had the good fortune to gain financial support from Eduard Conde, whose children he had taught. With Conde's financial assistance, Granados's goal of studying in Paris was realized. In September of 1887, Granados moved to Paris where he became the student of Charles-Wilfride de Bériot (1833–1914) at the Paris Conservatory. Although he maintained professional and personal ties with fellow musicians in Paris throughout his career, Granados's compositional style reflects more of the late-Romantic idiom with Spanish folk elements than any significant influence from the French school of composition.

After two years abroad and unable to interest Parisian publishers in his music, Granados returned to Barcelona and began what was to become a very successful career.

He arranged for the publication of his *12 Spanish Dances* with Casa Dotesio. Published in the early 1890s, the dances were praised by Edvard Grieg (1843–1907), Jules Massenet (1842–1912) and Camille Saint-Saëns (1835–1921). Performing frequently in concerts that included his original compositions, Granados established himself as a leading virtuoso, composer and teacher. In 1893, he married Amparo Gal y Lloberas, daughter of a Valencian businessman, Francesc Gal. They had six children: Eduardo, Soledad, Enrique, Victor, Francisco and Natalia. This last decade of the 19th century proved to be Granados's most productive years. Active as a soloist and collaborative pianist, Granados appeared frequently in concerts promoting chamber music in the essentially opera-oriented Spanish musical environment. He composed in many genres, including operettas, songs, chamber and orchestral works, and works for the piano. His 1898 operetta (*zarzuela*) *Maria del Carmen* was a qualified success and attracted the attention of the Queen Regent Maria Cristina who presented Granados with the Cross of Carlos III.

Concerned with the ineffectual state of music education in Spain (which he had personally experienced in his youth), in 1901 Granados founded and became the director of the Académia Granados in Barcelona. A brilliant pedagogue, his teaching philosophy was formulated on his own pedagogical principals and those of his illustrious teachers, Pujol and Bériot. The Academy offered music lessons in harmony, solfége, voice and piano. As a piano teacher, Granados stressed clarity, color, and performing in an expressive, improvisatory style with a mastery of the pedal. Many of these principles were discussed in his articles and books, and Granados came to be known as the father of the modern school of piano in Spain.

In 1898, during a visit to the Prado Art Museum in Madrid, Granados had the opportunity to view the paintings of Francisco Goya (1746–1828). He had previously seen some of Goya's paintings at the Louvre in Paris. Granados, who had always felt a kinship with his country's history, became increasingly fascinated with Goya's depiction of that picaresque Spanish period of political intrigues. His tribute to the great painter became a piano suite entitled *Goyescas*, which Granados performed for the first time in 1911. It is acknowledged as a masterpiece in the Spanish piano repertoire. The piano suite was expanded into an opera (also entitled *Goyescas*) and was accepted by the Paris Opera Company. However, due to the outbreak of World War I, the production was cancelled. By 1915, negotiations were finalized with the Metropolitan Opera Company of New York City for a scheduled January 28, 1916 performance of *Goyescas*. In November of 1915, Granados and his wife sailed to New York aboard the sea vessel *Montevideo*. During their stay in the city, Granados presented many concerts—including joint performances with the great cellist, Pablo Casals—and conducted public rehearsals of *Goyescas*. After the opera's premiere, Granados had planned to return home immediately. However, an invitation from the White House altered those plans and ultimately brought about disastrous results.

President Woodrow Wilson invited Granados to perform a concert at the White House. Accepting the President's invitation delayed Granados's return trip to Spain. After the White House concert, Granados rebooked his return passage to Spain by way of England. On March 11, 1916, Granados and his wife left New York on the *S.S. Rotterdam*. While in England, they visited friends and spent time pursuing the possibility of a London performance for *Goyescas*. Eager to return to Spain and their six children, they boarded the *S.S. Sussex* on March 24, 1916. While crossing the English Channel, the ship was torpedoed by the UB-29, a German submarine. Differing accounts describe the chaotic scene that ensued. It was reported that a French torpedo boat and several British destroyers were able to rescue 238 passengers, but Granados and his wife were among the 50 people who perished at sea. Ironically, Granados had a lifelong fear of water and a premonition of a "watery grave," which he had confessed to friends on many occasions. Memorial concerts were held in Spain, London, Paris and New York, in which some of the world's leading musicians performed, to benefit the six orphaned Granados children.

To this day, Granados's compositions, especially the *12 Spanish Dances*, continue to enthrall audiences worldwide.

ABOUT THE MUSIC

The publication of Granados's *12 Spanish Dances* coincided with the preparation for the 1892 Olympics, held on the great hill of Montjuïc, overlooking Barcelona. During the Olympics, one of the main attractions was an exhibit of Spanish villages that illustrated the diverse architectural styles and cultures found throughout the country's various regions. Granados had a similar concept in mind for his *12 Spanish Dances* by creating a cycle of keyboard vignettes depicting Spanish life.

Historians have claimed that Spanish music may be the richest in the world, due to the wide variety of civilizations that inhabited Spain. The great Spanish composer Manuel de Falla (1876–1946) claimed that the most important influences were the Byzantine, Moorish, Gypsy and Jewish cultures. Additionally, predating the Moors and the Gypsies, castanets were introduced in Spain by the ancient Greeks and Romans. Over a period of centuries, a musical fusion occurred, combining folk elements of all those cultures to create the Spanish idiom. During the Moorish occupation (711–1492), there were musical and cultural influences that profoundly affected Spanish music. However, by 1525, with the expulsion of the Moors and the prohibition of anything of Arabic origin, the lutes, bowed *rebecs* and tambourines used by the Moors were substituted for those instruments favored by the Gypsies. Utilizing the guitar, castanets, finger-snapping (*pitos*) and rhythmic hand-clapping (*palmadas*), the Gypsies developed the exotic *cante hondo* style, which later became the popular *cante flamenco* of today.

The flamenco idiom includes singing and has no strict choreography. Dancers improvise from basic movements, following the guitar and their own feelings. This free, spontaneous style suited Granados's innate proclivity for improvisation and originality. Granados created a pianistic style that combined elements of late Romanticism with folk idioms found in Spain's indigenous music. In addition to the rhythmic figurations imitative of castanets, Granados skillfully evoked guitaristic effects called *rasgueado* (strumming) and *punteado* (plucking). By utilizing indigenous dance rhythms—but not actual folk themes—he captured the spirit, character and the distinctive flavors of the diverse regions of Spain.

Songs and dances lie at the heart of Spanish music. The *12 Spanish Dances*, composed between 1887 and 1889, were the first works that gained Granados international recognition. Of the 12 dances, two are in $\frac{2}{4}$, one is in $\frac{6}{8}$, and the rest all carry a $\frac{3}{4}$ time signature. Sudden contrasts between major and minor evoke a common Moorish musical trait. The dances are characterized by clear tonal centers utilizing Hispano-Arab modes, dance-like rhythms, and expressive melodies that exhibit the chromatic inflection integral to the Andalucían folk cultures.

Granados was an advocate for artistic pedaling and spoke to his students about the "secrets of the pedal." As Spain's first modern piano pedagogue, his method book *Método, Teórico, Práctico* carefully documents many approaches for the proper use of the pedals. Varied pedaling allows for the artistic application of a full, half or quarter depression, as well as a delayed release that blends overlapping sonorities to create an acoustical blurring. The late Spanish pianist Alicia de Larrocha (1923–2009) referred to the latter pedal effect as "un poco borrado" (a little blurred). This special effect adds to the music's inherent mystique and exoticism. A gradually upward pedal release in slower passages and at the ends of phrases can also be musically effective.

PERFORMANCE NOTES

Granados's *12 Spanish Dances* begins with music reminiscent of the *style galant* spirit of the 18th century, which embodied formal elegance, lightness and simplicity. Dedicated to his wife Amparo Gal (prior to their marriage), Granados integrates Rococo elements and Spanish folk elements to create a stately minuet with a Spanish flavor. Spanish folk elements can be identified throughout the piece. Strong accents on the weak beats in measures 2, 4 and 8–10 allude to Spanish dancers' traditional *palmadas* (hand-clapping). Precise triplet figurations in measures 11, 12 and 23–25 suggest castanets. The use of opposing major and minor modes (a musical trait of the Moors) creates an exotic ambience (measures 26–29 in G major followed by measures 30–33 in G minor). In measures 26–33, the open fifths in the bass provide a drone effect, simulating the Spanish *gaita* (bagpipe).

The B section, beginning with measure 34, introduces a change of tempo and a brooding sadness with more drone effects in the bass. The piece transforms again at measure 42, with a tempo and mood change, as well as a more contrapuntal texture. A return to the exciting A section in measure 58 culminates in an exhilarating finale with music that radiates joy and optimism.

Historically, many civilizations inhabited Spain, producing great artistic benefits. In three-part form, "Oriental" conveys the exotic cultures of the Moors and the Gypsies who remained in Spain for centuries, dwelling largely in the southern region called Andalucía. Granados transports the listener back in time, evoking a Middle-Eastern ambience and retaining a classical simplicity, particularly in the A section (measures 1–47).

The B section (measures 48–66) is marked *lento assai*. Here, the plaintive melody exhibits an earthy quality, alluding to the music of the Gypsies as they soulfully proclaim their personal trials and sorrows. This passionate refrain (*copla*) evokes the expressive incantational style found in *cante hondo* and *cante flamenco*. In measures 49–51, the melody is embellished by one or more grace notes, suggesting castanets.

The *fandango* is a Spanish dance that appeared in Spain in the early 18th century. In moderate to fast triple time, it is traditionally danced by a couple, accompanied by castanets and guitar. Granados's "Fandango" alternates between elements of a lively dance (measures 1–4) and song-like elements (measures 5–8), which include fast grace notes simulating the sounds of castanets. Starting at measure 22, the staccato notes evoke the stamping of feet and heels (*taconeos*) accompanied by loud hand-clapping (*palmadas*) in the accented notes in measures 22–23 and 30–31. Phrases once again alternate between the elements of a dance (measures 37–44) and song-like elements (measures 45–52).

In measures 61–72, the boldness of the thematic material is interrupted by a contrapuntal variation that is in a slower tempo (designated *meno mosso*). These cantabile phrases express a serene ambience that, however fleeting, contrasts with the energetic dance theme that returns in measure 73. An exciting and technically difficult coda in measure 149 begins with an *allegro maestoso* tempo and reaches a joyously unrestrained fortissimo. This grand finale is reminiscent of a *jaleo*, in which spectators shout and loudly clap their hands, encouraging the dancers in their exhilarating performance.

Granados's late son Victor described this piece as follows: "The echo of a tender and captivating dance which brings the breeze from the far off mountains of old Castile and symbolizes a simple and happy pastoral scene." Granados found creative inspiration from Spain's cultural and musical heritage. The music of "Villanesca," with its gently flowing dance elements throughout the A sections, would represent most of Spain's regions. Nestled along the hillsides throughout Spain lie quaint country villages, with a church at each center. Imparting a spiritual quality to this bucolic scene, Granados imitates church bells with the repeated notes in measures 1–16, and continuing through most of the A sections. The B section at measure 83 is designated *canción y estribillo* (song and refrain). Here we find a *villancico*, an old Christian carol depicting the nativity scene and commonly found in the 17th-century version of the *villanesca*. Granados chooses a suitable Baroque contrapuntal texture for this beautiful middle section. The bass part of both A sections provides a drone effect, simulating the primitive Spanish *gaita* (bagpipe), which, for centuries, accompanied singers and dancers during the religious and festive occasions celebrated in Spain's small villages.

No. 5, Andaluza

"Andaluza" is a favorite piece among pianists and classical guitarists. The famous region of southern Spain known as Andalucía was inhabited by two colorful cultures—the Moors and the Gypsies. In this piece, Granados achieves the impression of an improvisation. In a Gypsy *cante flamenco* style, the bass in measures 1–3, 5–6 and throughout both A sections, has grace notes that hypnotically suggest the plucking sounds of the Arab *rebec*, a primitive stringed instrument. The character of this dance blends sorrow with joy, depicting the dichotomy of the Spanish soul. Granados employed opposing minor and major modes in measures 17–18, a Moorish musical trait. Measure 18 introduces a change in spirit, climactically reaching fortissimo at the first chord in measure 22. It would be stylistically appropriate to lengthen its value with an agogic accent.

Frequent accent marks, as in measures 4 and 7, bring to mind the sensuous picture of a Gypsy dancer's hand-clapping (*palmadas*). In measures 11–12, the repeated bass notes suggest the *punteado* (plucking) effect of a guitar. A fragment of the principle theme in rhythmic augmentation cleverly signals the contrasting B section (measures 32–64), which alternates expressive song-like phrases (measures 32–39) with phrases suggestive of a guitar (measures 39–47). This edition offers the composer's

final revisions for this piece. "Andaluza" is a priceless Spanish treasure. It is a musical masterpiece that magically invokes the fiery spirit, tenderness and passion of Spanish music.

No. 6, Rondalla Aragonesa

Granados's late son Victor described this piece as "an impression of a local festival in the valley of Anso…a description of the atmosphere of a *rondalla*…in which singing and dancing stand out." Granados was inspired by folklore and Spain's indigenous folk music. The dance represented in this piece is a *jota* originating from the region of Aragón. Spain has a wealth of national dances and the *jota* is its most famous. In moderate to rapid triple time, it is performed by one or more couples facing each other, holding castanets at arm's length, and moving back and forth in a seemingly hostile manner. Ironically, it traditionally expresses the theme of courtship. The music of a *rondalla* would include singers, dancers, castanets and guitar. With a pulsating rhythm and a steadily increasing tempo, the dance is exhilarating. This piece requires solid technical command as the music intensifies and the tempo grows ever faster. The A sections exhibit the excitement of the dance with the initial theme of measures 1–12 becoming more intense as it adds more thematic variants.

Guitar effects of the *rasgueado* (strumming) technique are suggested in the arpeggiated chords of measures 12, 16 and 36. Tempo changes typical of the Spanish idiom lead into the very expressive *copla*, the B section of measures 74–105. Here Granados provides contrasting instrumental phrases, setting the expressive mood for the *canto* or song. The *canto* appears in the soprano voice with a short phrase in measure 75, followed by a longer *canto* at measures 77–81. In measure 87, the first note in the right hand can be played with an agogic accent by lengthening its duration for expressive intent. The grace notes in measures 75, 79 and 83 suggest the sounds of castanets. This brilliant piece requires the pianist's total commitment to performing with an endearing musicality for an authentic and an artistic interpretation.

No. 7, Valenciana

"Valenciana" artistically depicts the vibrant musical life in Valencia, the third largest city on the southeastern seacoast of Spain. The city was founded by the Romans in 138 B.C., later conquered by the Moors, and retaken for the Christians in 1094 by the nobleman Rodrigo Diaz de Vivar (ca. 1043–1099). Because of his heroism, the Moors named Vivar "El Cid," from the Arabic for "Lord." Now a modern city, Valencia's historical past served as the creative inspiration for Granados's composition. "Valenciana" displays some of the musical elements of a *jota*, a dance from the region of Aragón. Granados performed this piece as an encore for his concert at the White House, and referred to it as the "Jota Valenciana." Spanish dance genres often assumed regional adaptations. In measures 1–3, guitar-like passages are interspersed with lyrical phrases (measures 4–7). The tempo indication of *Allegro airoso* connotes a lively, jaunty spirit. Famed Spanish pianist Alicia de Larrocha would often say: "The left hand is more important than the right. It is like a column that holds the whole building." The triplet figurations suggestive of castanets (measures 8–10 and similar places) are contrasted by bold vocal declamations (measures 12–13). The strumming guitar technique of *rasgueado* (measures 14–17) is suggested frequently through the arpeggiated chords.

The development of the initial musical phrases builds in intensity by the gradual addition of notes and moving toward higher-pitched tonal centers. The melodic theme in measure 12 is transformed in measure 48 in the bass and again in measure 56 in the treble. A second theme in measures 18 and 19 finds a melodic modulation in measures 40 and 41. Measures 63–78 provide an interlude (designated *poco più mosso)* and feature a virtuosic display of guitars and dancers, accompanied by castanets. Measures 102–109 and 158–165 exhibit a hostility that rhythmically suggests galloping horses. The exhilarating dance draws to a close with a coda at measure 171. An unexpected *Andante* tempo bids us a tender farewell. This edition offers Granados's final revisions for this great piece, elevating it to even higher levels of artistic achievement.

The northern province of Asturias, where fertile landscapes and snow-capped mountains descend to the Cantabrian Sea, is rich in folklore and pride. Surrounded by mountain ranges, the people from Asturias have been characterized as possessing a determined and indomitable spirit. The rugged terrain proved impenetrable for the Moors, who attempted an invasion in 714. A Visigoth nobleman named Pelayo, leading a small band of men and vastly outnumbered, defeated the army of the Moors. An immense statue of Pelayo is visible near the battle site in The National Park of Covadonga, with his gaze defiantly directed toward the surrounding mountains.

In "Asturiana," Granados establishes a sense of monumental grandeur and bold virility by selecting sonorities from the lowest to the highest registers of the piano, possibly a musical depiction of the region's topography. In measures 1–36 (and again in measures 72–118), the music ascends to precipitous heights reaching a *ffff* in measure 118. The C mixolydian mode (a C major scale with a flatted 7th), provides the appropriate exotic ambience in the A sections. At measure 37, there is a change of tempo to *più mosso* for the B section. The phrases in this mid-section vary from a rapid equestrian spirit of urgency, as in measures 37–45, to moments of repose with song-like elements, in measures 46–48. Measures 66, 70, and 71 rhythmically suggest the ominous presence of horses at a fast gallop. These changes of tempo and mood require artistic handling and the use of rubato for expressive freedom. The rhythmic sounds of castanets are evident in the numerous grace notes that contribute flashes of color. Measure 72 announces the return of an expanded A section, permeating the landscape with an exuberant and celebratory spirit.

Granados composed in a very expressive and improvisatory style, reflecting a late-Romantic propensity. As a pianist, he favored and performed works by Chopin, Grieg and other composers from that era of Romanticism. "Romántica," set in $\frac{3}{4}$ meter with a tempo indication of *Molto allegro brillante*, displays the characteristics of a mazurka. The mazurka, a folk dance of Polish origin, spread throughout Europe in the 18th and 19th centuries—first as a dance, and later as a source of art music. "Romántica" is a highly stylized piece that includes musical components of the dance, yet also incorporates characteristics of the Spanish folk idiom.

Measures 1–50 are bold and assertive with changes of tempo. At measure 51, a contrasting dance-like theme is introduced, featuring grace notes and triplet figures, suggestive of castanets. Measures 67–83 transform this dance theme into octave passages with great dynamic excitement. Measures 87–122 introduce a song-like theme in the exotic B-flat mixolydian mode. At measure 87, Granados infuses the landscape with a

Spanish flavor by including a light dance-like theme in measures 93–95, followed by a virtuosic guitar-like flourish in measure 98. In measures 171–172 and 180–181, Granados creates a charming digression with a bass chromaticism characteristic of the mazurkas. Measures 185–219 return to the soulful music with Spanish flavor and a final dramatic statement. In his last revision of the closing measures of "Romántica," Granados tosses up colorful fireworks with a final flourish of artistic brilliance.

The music of "Melancólica" represents the southern region of Spain called Andalucía, known for *cante flamenco*. Granados's compositional procedure was to suggest—rather than to copy—the sounds of guitars and castanets, using specific dance rhythms with his own melodies. In flamenco, dancers improvise from basic movements, following the guitar and their feelings. This spontaneous freedom appealed to Granados's proclivity for improvisation.

This piece includes features of the exciting heel-stamping solo dance known as a *zapateado*. Granados brings frequent changes in tempo, which achieves an expressive intent. Measure 43 begins at *meno mosso*, but is soon followed by an *accelerando* and a guitaristic flourish at measures 46–47. The B section (measures 57–71) is performed cantabile with expressive rubato. The melancholic mood culminates in measure 68 with a climactic fortissimo. At this dynamic level, an agogic accent lengthening the duration of the note will heighten the dramatic effect. With the inclusion of a seemingly improvised flourish, the exhilarating dance commences at measure 72, signaling a return of the A section.

In the region of southern Spain known as Andalucía, the Moors built magnificent palaces for their festive celebrations. In Granada, "La Alhambra," which was completed in the 14th century, is the largest remaining Moorish palace in Spain. It is famous for its architectural greatness and its beauty. "Arabesque," with its haunting charm, evokes a celebratory dance called a *zambra*, which means "revelry by night." Granados creates a mysterious setting for his musical depiction. A plaintive two-measure phrase suggesting the sounds of an Arab *nay*, an ancient vertical flute, invites us to enter.

The A sections provide exotic melodies artistically decorated with grace notes (measures 2–10), musically resembling the intricate ornamental stuccowork (or *arabesques*) found in the Moorish palaces. These melodic embellishments also suggest the plucking sound of the Arab *rebec*, a primitive stringed instrument. Changes of mood heighten the drama and suspense in measures 12–24, rhythmically displaying a spirited, equestrian-like energy. The B section (*copla*) of measures 39–71 expresses intense sorrow, despair and supplication. The modality of this section is similar to D phrygian with a raised 3rd (D, E-flat, F-sharp, G, A, B-flat, C and D). This is also the mode derived from the fifth step of the harmonic minor scale. This colorful modality provides an exotic ambience for the soulful outpouring of emotion. While many of Granados's early works end with the final cadence on the dominant, this is the only piece in the set of *12 Spanish Dances* that employs this effect.

At the heart of Spanish music rests its songs and dances, which were integral to the cultures that settled in Spain. For Granados's final bow in the completion of his *12 Spanish Dances*, he chose a bolero for piece No. 12. The A sections provide rhythmic dance steps in the treble with grace notes in the bass (as seen in measures 1–10) suggesting the sounds of *pitos* (finger snaps) and a guitar accompaniment. The treble grace notes in measures 4, 6, 7 and 8 suggest the sound of castanets. The dance becomes more exhilarating in measures 11–20 with accented chords implying fast feet stamping and vigorous *palmadas* (hand clapping).

The B section (measures 49–71) begins with one measure of an accentuated vocal declamation designated *marcato il canto*, alternating with phrases of repose (as in measures 50, 52, 54, etc.) This simulates the sudden stops and pauses typical of a *bolero*. The music reaches an emotional zenith at measure 62. An agogic accent on the first note of that measure will appropriately heighten the dramatic effect. "Bolero" is a musical depiction of *cuadro flamenco*, which includes dancers, singers and guitarists sitting in a semi-circle, and audience members clapping and shouting comments (*jaleos*) after each well-executed step. In measure 100, the indication *lusingando* (caressingly) signifies a tender farewell. With the final measure, Granados's *12 Spanish Dances* ends elegantly, yet simply, with a magical two-note finger snap.

ABOUT THIS EDITION

The *12 Spanish Dances* were first published circa 1890 by Casa Dotesio of Barcelona, and were subsequently reprinted by the Unión Musical Española. Facsimiles of the first Spanish printing served as the text for this edition. All past editions follow the imperfect first printing, which was replete with engravers' errors. The first printing also lacked the interpretive details integral for the stylistic performance practice tradition of Spanish music. The Unión Musical Española edition is considered the primary source for Dances Nos. 1–9. The primary source for Dances Nos. 10–12, with revisions made by Granados, is designated as Unión Musical Española—UME-G (G for Granados).

The editor conducted research in Madrid's Real Conservatorio de la Música, the Biblioteca Nacional in Madrid, and the Museu de la Música in Barcelona. She also consulted Granados's book entitled *Método, Teórico, Práctico*, as well as *Estudio Práctico Sobre los Pedales del Piano* and *La Sonoridad del Piano* by Granados's student/disciple, Frank Marshall. The editor studied with the renowned pianist Alicia de Larrocha at the Acadèmia Marshall in Barcelona, and privately over a period of 30 years. Dr. de Larrocha provided the Spanish legacy regarding the performance practice tradition of Granados's music, which also involved Granados's revisions and changes, made evident from his performances on the Welte-Mignon and Duo-Art piano rolls. Granados revised and refined the 12 *Spanish Dances*, sharing his revisions with Frank Marshall, the teacher/mentor of Alicia de Larrocha.

EDITORIAL CONSIDERATIONS

This is the first critical edition published in the United States that includes Granados's final revisions. The original edition with Granados's written changes, published by Unión Musical Española, can be found in the Archivo Alicia de Larrocha, Barcelona. These changes made by the composer reveal a more refined version of his compositions by sustaining certain notes, creating different rhythmic patterns, and adding new melodic phrases and new endings.

In this edition, parenthetical material and pedaling are editorial. Fingering is also editorial, as well as some redistribution of notes between the hands to improve technical facility. Artistic refinements, integral to the stylistic performance of Spanish music, have also been added by the editor. This includes modifications of the tempo to highlight interchange between lyrical and instrumental phrases. This editor's objective was to assist pianists in achieving an authentic and artistic interpretation, thereby preserving the performance practice tradition of Granados's music.

TITLES

According to Alicia de Larrocha, Granados gave titles to only two of the *12 Spanish Dances*—No. 4, "Villanesca" and No. 7, "Valenciana." The titles for the remaining pieces were assigned by the music publisher. After Granados's death, titles were changed for seven of the pieces:

No. 1, "Minueto" became "Galante"

No. 3, "Zarabanda" became "Fandango"

No. 8, "Asturiana" became "Sardana"

No. 9, "Mazurka" became "Romántica"

No. 10, "Danza Triste" became "Melancólica"

No. 11, "Zambra" became "Arabesca"

No. 12, "Arabesca" became "Bolero"

This editor adhered to the title changes with the exception of No. 8, "Asturiana," which was renamed "Sardana," after the national dance of the Catalán region. This editor's rationale for retaining the original title of "Asturiana" is due to the musical components of the composition that pointedly evoke the idiographic characteristics of the northern Asturias-Cantabrian region, which also happens to have been the birthplace of Granados's mother.

GLOSSARY OF SPANISH TERMS

Andalucía—the southern region of Spain comprising the cities of Almería, Cádiz, Córdoba, Granada, Huelva, Jaén, Málaga and Sevilla. The region is known for its *cante flamenco* (see definition below).

bolero—a Spanish dance in $\frac{3}{4}$ time invented circa 1780 by Sebastian Cerezo, a celebrated dancer of Cádiz. It is performed by either one dancer or a couple, accompanied by castanets. The dance includes many intricate steps with stamping of the feet, very abrupt pauses, and frequent tempo fluctuations.

cante hondo (cante jondo)—of Byzantine and Jewish origin, *cante hondo* is a melancholy song with repetition of short phrases, an absence of strict meter, expressive ornamentation and a tragic mood. It is often found in the middle section of ternary forms, or presented intermittently around dance-like passages.

cante flamenco—a song style developed from early 19th-century *cante hondo* with Middle Eastern influences. By the late 19th century, Gypsies adopted the *cante hondo*, renaming it *cante flamenco*.

copla—a stanza or refrain of the *cante hondo*. The Andalucían *copla* is intensely passionate.

cuadro flamenco—an ensemble that includes dancers, singers and guitarists sitting in a semi-circle.

flamenco—stylistic performances of folk songs and dances accompanied by guitar and castanets, particularly represented in southern Spain's Andalucían region.

jaleos—loud hand-clapping and shouted words of encouragement from spectators during an Andalucían dance.

jota—originating from the region of Aragón, a *jota* is a dance in moderate to rapid triple time. Traditionally it expressed the theme of courtship.

La Alhambra—the palace in Granada built by the Moors, the mixed Arab and Berber conquerors of Spain. Its architectural beauty provided Granados with creative inspiration.

palmadas—rhythmic hand-clapping of dancers.

pitos—finger snaps accompanying Gypsy dancers, traditionally favored over the castanets by artistic purists.

punteado—a common guitar technique of plucking the strings with the right-hand fingertips, to play individual notes in succession.

rasgueado—a common guitar technique of strumming the strings to produce chordal effects and arpeggios.

taconeos—Spanish dancers' stamping heels and feet.

zapateado—a Spanish dance in triple time in which the performer engages in rapid stamping of the heels.

zarzuela—a Spanish operetta with spoken dialogue, singing and dancing. It is named after La Zarzuela, the palace outside Madrid where, in the 17th century, comedians presented short programs before King Philip IV.

ACKNOWLEDGEMENTS

Grateful appreciation is extended to editors E.L. Lancaster and Carol Matz for contributing their professional expertise to this edition.

12 SPANISH DANCES

Galante

Enrique Granados (1867–1916)
Op. 5, No. 1

Oriental

Op. 5, No. 2

Fandango

Op. 5, No. 3

(a) In measures 19 and 27, the grace note can be played simultaneously with the octave.

Villanesca

Op. 5, No. 4

Andaluza

Op. 5, No. 5

Andantino quasi Allegretto

Rondalla Aragonesa

Op. 5, No. 6

Tempo I, *poco a poco accelerando*

Valenciana

Op. 5, No. 7

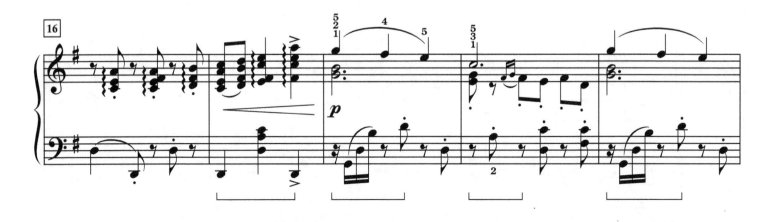

Asturiana

Op. 5, No. 8

Romántica

Op. 5, No. 9

Molto allegro brillante

(a) The pedal throughout this piece combines sonorities that create the *un poco borrado* (a little blurred) effect.

62

Melancólica

Op. 5, No. 10

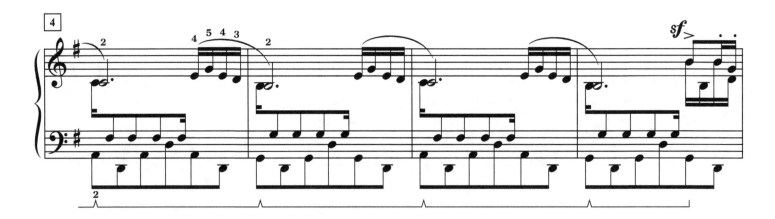

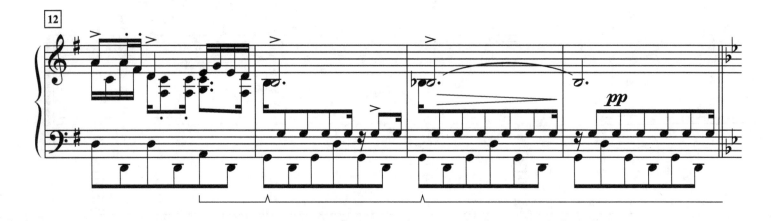

Arabesca

Op. 5, No. 11

Largo a piacere

Andante con moto

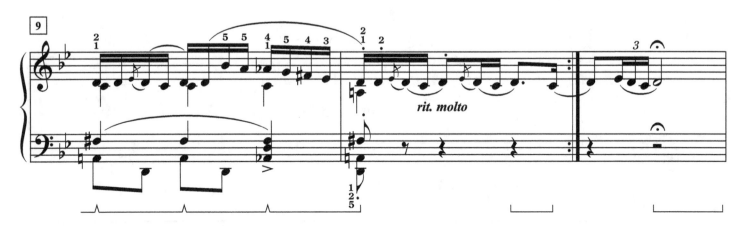

72

73

74

76

Bolero

Op. 5, No. 12

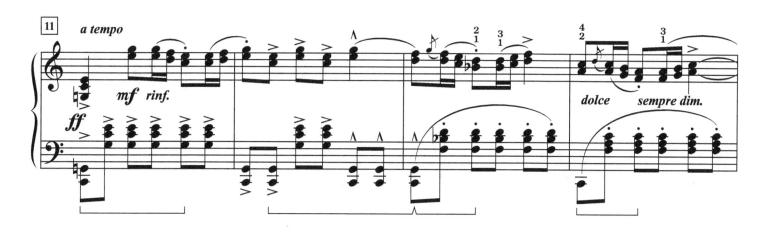